THE AMERICAN GIRLS

  KAYA, an adventurous Nez Perce girl whose deep love for horses and respect for nature nourish her spirit

  FELICITY, a spunky, spritely colonial girl, full of energy and independence

  JOSEFINA, a Hispanic girl whose heart and hopes are as big as the New Mexico sky

  KIRSTEN, a pioneer girl of strength and spirit who settles on the frontier

  ADDY, a courageous girl determined to be free in the midst of the Civil War

  SAMANTHA, a bright Victorian beauty, an orphan raised by her wealthy grandmother

1934 KIT, a clever, resourceful girl facing the Great Depression with spirit and determination

1944 MOLLY, who schemes and dreams on the home front during World War Two

1974 JULIE, a fun-loving girl from San Francisco who faces big changes—and creates a few of her own

1974

Julie AND THE EAGLES

By MEGAN MCDONALD

ILLUSTRATIONS ROBERT HUNT

VIGNETTES SUSAN McALILEY

★ American Girl®

Published by American Girl Publishing, Inc.
Copyright © 2007 by American Girl, LLC
All rights reserved. No part of this book may be used or reproduced in
any manner whatsoever without written permission except in the case of
brief quotations embodied in critical articles and reviews.

Questions or comments? Call 1-800-845-0005, visit **americangirl.com**,
or write to Customer Service, American Girl, 8400 Fairway Place,
Middleton, WI 53562-0497.

Printed in China
07 08 09 10 11 12 LEO 10 9 8 7 6 5 4 3 2 1

All American Girl marks, Julie™, and Julie Albright™
are trademarks of American Girl, LLC.

PICTURE CREDITS
The following individuals and organizations have generously
given permission to reprint images contained in "Looking Back":
p. 59—© J. P. Laffont/Sygma/Corbis; pp. 60–61—Jupiter Images
(crossing stream); © Underwood & Underwood/Corbis (Rachel Carson);
The Riverside Press, Cambridge (Silent Spring); Getty Images (banner);
© Bettmann/Corbis (cleaning sidewalks); pp. 62–63—Picturequest (bald eagle);
© J. P. Laffont/Sygma/Corbis (chalk writing); Photo by Linda Cyrek for Back to the Wild,
Castalia, OH, courtesy of Mona Rutger (wildlife rescue worker);
© Galen Rowell/Corbis (spotted owl); © Dan Lamont/Corbis (logger);
pp. 64–65—© Shaun Walker (Julia Butterfly Hill); © Joel W. Rogers/Corbis (clearcut);
© Tom Stewart/Corbis (girl on peak).

Cataloging-in-Publication Data available from Library of Congress

FOR MY SISTERS

TABLE OF CONTENTS

JULIE'S FAMILY AND FRIENDS

JULIE'S FAMILY

JULIE
*A girl full of energy
and new ideas, trying to
find her place in
times of change*

TRACY
*Julie's trendy
teenage sister, who is
sixteen years old*

MOM
*Julie's artistic
mother, who runs
a small store*

DAD
*Julie's father,
an airline pilot who flies
all over the world*

IVY
*Julie's best friend,
who loves doing
gymnastics*

T.J.
*A boy at school
who plays basketball
with Julie*

CHAPTER ONE

A CRY IN THE PARK

Conservatory of Flowers

Julie Albright picked up the phone and called her best friend. "Ivy, you have to come over right away. I'm sick!"

"What do you have?" Ivy asked.

"Spring fever!" Julie practically shouted.

While Julie waited for her friend to be dropped off, she scrubbed her sister Tracy's old bike and her own. The pink and chrome gleamed in the early April sunshine. Julie pumped air into the tires as Ivy hopped out of her mom's car.

Ivy pointed to streaks of grease under Julie's eyes. "You look like a raccoon," she teased.

"Make that grease monkey," said Julie. She

1

straightened the wicker basket on the front. "I want to get one of those Snoopy bike horns for my birthday."

"Your birthday's still a month away," said Ivy.

"Twenty-eight days, to be exact," said Julie. "I can't wait to turn double digits. I'll finally be as old as you." Ivy laughed.

"So, want to ride bikes to Golden Gate Park?" Julie asked. "Mom told me the gardens by the Conservatory have ten thousand tulips and they're all blooming!" The park was just two blocks away.

"Hey, maybe we can get a snow cone, too. I have three dollars left over from my Chinese New Year money," said Ivy.

The girls took off up the hill, their bright pink bike tassels flapping in the wind. They entered the park on a path near the stadium, where picnickers sat on blankets in the grass and teenagers tossed Frisbees. Julie and Ivy swerved when a terrier ran across the path, yipping at their wheels. The girls laughed, speeding toward the Conservatory, a huge greenhouse with an elegant dome like a glass palace. All around it, a sea of purple tulips and yellow daffodils nodded in the spring breeze.

"I've never seen so many flowers," said Ivy. "It smells sweeter than strawberry bubble bath."

"Look at the hummingbird!" said Julie, hopping off her bike. A green flash of wings zoomed here, there, and back again. The girls sat in the cool grass, people-watching and soaking up the spring sunshine. A guy with a ponytail played a flute, a large hairy dog pulled a kid on roller skates, and a woman in a peasant dress sold crystals to passersby.

"Hold still. Don't move," Ivy whispered. "A butterfly just landed on your shoulder."

Julie sat as still as stone, moving only her eyes to get a peek. The butterfly had iridescent blue-lavender wings outlined in black.

"Oh my! That's a mission blue butterfly." Julie squinted up to see a white-haired lady smiling back from under the wide brim of a straw hat. Her blue eyes sparkled in a face full of wrinkles. "I couldn't help noticing your new little friend there," said the lady.

"Maybe it thinks you're a flower," said Ivy.

"I've never seen a blue butterfly before," said Julie, watching the butterfly float away.

"That's because they're becoming quite rare. But

Julie sat as still as a stone, moving only her eyes to get a peek.

they love the lupine garden here." The lady nodded toward the tall, showy spikes of purple, pink, and yellow blooms across the path from the tulip garden. "When I was a girl, we used to go on walks through Muir Woods, and we saw mission blues everywhere. Too bad we don't see more of them nowadays. It was a real treat to see one today." The lady smiled and turned to go. "Nice talking with you girls."

"Bye!" Julie and Ivy called, waving after her as she headed down the pebbled path.

"How about that snow cone?" Julie asked. The girls walked their bikes over to the cart where a vendor called, "Get your snow cones here. Blue raspberry, lemon, lime, watermelon!"

"What can I get for you girls today?" he asked, scooping up a ball of crushed ice and filling a paper cone.

"Do we have to pick one flavor?" Julie asked. "Or can we get rainbow?"

"Rainbow it is, coming right up," said the man, squirting red, blue, green, and yellow syrup onto the ball of ice.

"Make that two," said Ivy.

The girls steered their bikes toward a bench

under some shade trees, where they slurped their icy treats.

"What's that noise?" Julie asked, looking around.

"That's me slurping," said Ivy.

"No, I mean that little squeak. Hear it?" Both girls craned their necks toward the grove of trees behind their bench.

"There—look," said Julie, jumping up. "I saw something move under that pink bush." The girls stood as still as statues. They did not hear a peep.

"Maybe we scared it," said Julie.

Weep, weep.

Julie looked at Ivy. Ivy looked at Julie. Their eyes grew wide. "There it is again," Julie whispered.

"I heard it, too," Ivy said.

"Sounds like a baby bird," said Julie. The girls peered under the azalea bush. Julie blinked. A pair of round yellow eyes blinked back at her.

"A baby owl!" she whispered. It was no bigger than a tennis ball, with pointy ear tufts and a sharp hooked beak. It was covered with downy gray fuzz as soft as dandelion fluff.

"Where's your mama?" Ivy asked.

"Maybe it's hurt," said Julie. "It must have fallen

6

out of a nest. It's too young to fly." She peered up at the treetops, looking for a nest. "I don't see anything that looks like a nest."

"Even if we did find a nest, how would we get the baby back up into it?" Ivy asked. "And I don't hear a mama owl calling."

"All I hear are those noisy crows," said Julie, glancing at the black birds circling overhead. "They might come after it. We have to save it."

"Can't the mama owl come save it?" Ivy asked.

"What if it's lost? We can't just leave it here—a cat or a dog or a raccoon could find it." Julie untied her sweatshirt from around her waist. She turned it inside out to make a soft bed and set it under the bush next to the owl. "C'mon, little one," she coaxed. "Hop into my sweatshirt and we'll take you home."

The baby bird didn't move.

"Something's wrong with it," said Ivy.

Cupping her hand under the baby owl, Julie lifted it into the soft sweatshirt and eased it out from under the bush. The girls stood a moment, in awe of the small creature.

"Don't be scared," Julie whispered. "We'll take care of you." Carefully, she settled the bird in the

basket on the front of her bike. The baby
owl nestled down into the folds, as if it
were being tucked into bed.

"Aw, he's sooooo cute!" said Ivy.
"Look at all that soft, fluffy fuzz."

"Let's get you home, fuzz face," Julie cooed. She
hopped on her bike and was just about to push off
when she froze. "Wait a minute. We can't take it to
my apartment. Pets aren't allowed. You'll have to
take it home to your house."

"I can't," said Ivy. "We have two cats, remember?
The bird would last about two seconds around
Jasmine and Wonton."

"And I can't take it to Dad's house, since I'm
only there on weekends, and he's away a lot." Julie
twisted the hem of her shirt, thinking.

Ivy grabbed Julie's arm and pointed. "Look,
there's that nice lady who told us about the
butterflies. Maybe she knows about birds, too."

"Good idea," said Julie. They wheeled their bikes
across the grass to the lady, who was bent over
sniffing a bright red azalea.

"Excuse me," said Julie.

The woman looked up. "Oh, hello again, girls."

"We found a baby owl," said Julie, parting the folds of her sweatshirt to show the lady. "We heard it crying. We couldn't find its mother or see a nest and we thought we shouldn't leave it there all alone, but we don't know what to do."

"Looks to me like you've found a baby screech owl. They don't build nests—they live in holes in trees."

"No wonder we couldn't see any nest," said Ivy.

"Poor thing's trembling," said the woman. "It must have fallen out of a tree."

"What should we do?" Julie asked.

"It needs help right away," the lady said. "Do you girls know where the Randall Museum is? It's not far from the park. They have a rescue center there. They can take care of injured wild animals."

"It's just a few blocks from my house," said Julie. "I've passed by there lots of times."

"I'm sure they'll know what to do," said the lady.

"Thanks," Julie and Ivy called, hopping back on their bikes. Julie cooed to the little owl all the way out of the park, down Waller Street, and up the hill to the museum.

Randall Museum

C H A P T E R
T W O
—

FEATHERED
FRIENDS

At the Randall Museum, Julie and Ivy introduced themselves to a young woman with long brown hair who was wearing hiking boots, khaki pants, and a college sweatshirt.

"Hi, I'm Robin Young," she said. "Let's see what you've got there."

Julie held out the sweatshirt nest. She and Ivy told Robin all about finding the baby owl.

"Let's take a look at this little guy." Robin set the bundle down on a table in the workroom. "Looks like a baby screech owl, probably only a week or two old."

"Do you think it's going to be okay?" asked Julie.

"You did the right thing to keep it warm and

safe. Most of the time it's best to leave wild creatures alone, but in this case, there's no way this little guy would have made it through the night in the park."

Pulling on gloves, she gently turned the baby owl onto its back.

The owl's head was twitching, and its eyes blinked nonstop.

"Is it scared?" Julie asked.

"Probably." Robin frowned. "Has it been blinking and twitching like this since you found it?"

"Yes," Julie said.

"That's not a good sign," said Robin. "Rapid blinking and head twitching can mean that the bird's been poisoned."

"Who would poison a baby bird?" asked Ivy.

"Nobody poisoned it on purpose. Most likely, it ate something containing pesticides, like DDT."

"What's DDT?" Julie asked.

"A chemical," Robin explained. "Farmers used to spray it on their fields and orchards so that insects wouldn't eat all their crops. Then birds swallowed it when they ate the leaves or insects. A law was passed to stop the use of DDT a few years ago, but we still see the effects of it moving up the food chain."

"Do you think you can save the owl?" Julie asked.

"We'll know in the next forty-eight hours," said Robin. "For now, I'll get out a heating pad to keep it nice and warm, give it water every fifteen minutes, and see if I can get the little guy to eat a mealworm."

"Can I come back and visit him?" Julie asked.

"Sure, any time," said Robin. "I'm a graduate student at Berkeley, but I'm here most days when I'm not in class."

"Thanks," said Julie. "I'll be back tomorrow."

The next day after school, Julie set off for the museum.

"Hi! Remember me?" she asked Robin.

"Of course," said Robin. "But I'm sorry to say the little owl isn't here. We were afraid it might not make it through the night, so we took it to the vet late yesterday, where it can get around-the-clock care. The vet says the owl made it through the night, so that's a hopeful sign."

"Oh, that's good." But Julie couldn't hide her disappointment at not getting to see the owl again.

"Well, no sense coming here today for nothing," said Robin. "Would you like to meet Shasta and Sierra and their babies?"

"Shasta and Sierra? Are they owls, too?"

"You'll see," said Robin, smiling as if she had a surprise. She led Julie back to a cage the size of a small room. Perched side by side on a large branch were two huge brown eagles with snow-white heads and shiny yellow beaks. Their bright yellow eyes fixed Julie and Robin with a stern gaze.

"Meet Shasta and Sierra, our national symbols," Robin said with a note of pride.

Julie gasped in amazement. She had seen pictures of bald eagles before, but that hadn't prepared her for the sheer size and majesty of these two birds. "I never knew birds could look so intelligent—or so fierce," she whispered.

Robin pointed toward the back of the cage. "See that heap of sticks up on the shelf in back? That's a makeshift nest that we made out of twigs and lined with pine needles. And those two gray fuzzy lumps

13

are Shasta and Sierra's babies."

Julie peered through the wire
mesh. Standing on tiptoe, she could
just see two downy heads sticking up
out of the nest. They looked like
speckled balls of lint from the dryer.
"They don't look anything like their parents. They
have dark eyes and dark heads," Julie noted.

"They're about four weeks old, still nestlings.
They're just starting to get their first feathers."

"Aw," said Julie. "Did they hatch right here at the
rescue center?"

"Yep," said Robin. "It was amazing to watch.
But we have to keep a close eye on them. Shasta
and Sierra are stressed by being in captivity. They're
used to hunting and fishing in the wild. They don't
always know how to take care of their babies in a
confined space."

Julie stood mesmerized. As she watched, one of
the adult eagles hopped onto a perch only a few feet
away from her.

"That's Shasta," said Robin. "You can tell
because the male's a bit smaller than the female."

Up close, Julie saw that Shasta's right wing was

bandaged. "What happened to him?" she asked.

"We're not exactly sure," said Robin. "The eagles came to us from Marin County, where trees were being cleared to make room for new houses. We think the tree that held their nest was cut down. Some construction workers found Shasta flapping one wing on the ground, unable to fly. Sierra, his mate, was nearby."

"When his wing heals up, will you be able to let them go?" Julie asked.

"We want to," said Robin. "But the museum doesn't have the funding for an eagle release."

"You mean you can't just let them go outside?"

"No," Robin said with a sigh. "A bald eagle release takes a lot of preparation—and a lot of money. Before we can release them, we need to build a hack tower, and—"

"A hack tower?" Julie asked.

"A platform about forty feet above the ground—as high as an eagle's nest," Robin explained. "It gives the eagles a safe place where they'll have food and shelter for a few months, until they get used to hunting and building

hack tower

nests again in the wild. We'd be working with the Fish and Wildlife Service. They band the eagles and keep track of them and feed them. And somebody has to get paid to do all that."

Julie frowned. "Can't the museum pay to build the tower and everything?"

"It costs at least a thousand dollars, and we just don't have that kind of money. The Randall is a small museum. We run mostly on donations and volunteers, and we have other animals to care for, too." Robin shook her head. "The sad part is, if the eagles are in captivity much longer, it'll be too late—they won't be able to adapt back to the wild."

"What will happen if they can't go back into the wild?"

"They'll have to live at a zoo," said Robin.

"Even the baby eagles?" Julie asked.

"We can't let the eaglets go without their parents to feed them. And one of the babies isn't doing well. Shasta and Sierra seem confused in this cage, and they sometimes neglect to feed their babies."

Julie looked into Shasta's intense yellow eyes

and shivered. She could sense the wildness in him. She couldn't bear the thought of him spending the rest of his life in a cage.

CHAPTER
THREE
—
ENDANGERED

"I love driving!" Tracy crowed as she and Julie left the Golden Gate Bridge behind and headed toward the rainbow tunnel. "It was okay driving around the high school parking lot with Dad on Sundays, but it's much more fun having my license."

"Now you can take me everywhere," Julie joked.

"Tell me again why you need me to drive you to the middle of nowhere?" Tracy asked.

"It's a place in Marin County where they're building new houses," said Julie, glancing down again at the paper with the directions Robin had given her. "It's where the bald eagles were found. The builders cut down hundreds of tall trees. It's their fault that Shasta and Sierra are living in a cage now."

When Julie saw a big sign saying Mountain Meadow Homes, she told Tracy to pull off the highway. A rutted dirt road led up to a construction trailer. Nervously, Julie peeked in the open door. A man in jeans, work boots, and a flannel shirt was bent over blueprints. "Excuse me," said Julie, stepping inside. "Are you the man in charge?"

"I'm the foreman," he said, peering over his glasses. "I'm just guessing you're not the new backhoe operator."

"No, I'm Julie Albright, and this is my sister—"

"—and you're lost."

"No!" said Julie. "I came to talk to you about—about bald eagles." The foreman raised his eyebrows and waited for her to continue.

"You're cutting down trees where they have their nests," she went on.

He rolled his eyes. "Don't tell me you're one of those tree huggers."

"What's a tree hugger?"

The foreman gave her a thin smile. "Somebody who cares more about trees than people."

"I care about people," Julie said, standing up straighter. "But I care about eagles, too. And you're cutting down so many trees, the eagles have nowhere left to live."

He pinched the bridge of his nose. "Now they're sending me eight-year-olds to pull on the heartstrings."

"For your information, I'm nine, and I'll be ten in a few weeks," Julie replied.

"My mistake. Look, kid, I'm busy. I've got homes to build. And no pipsqueak is gonna shut down this work site."

Julie looked at Tracy, who nudged her, urging her on. She took a deep breath.

"All I know is, because of you, some wild bald eagles have to spend the rest of their lives in a cage unless we get some money to save them. Can't you help?"

"Listen, missy, we had an environmental impact study done before we broke ground on this project. And nobody said one word about any bald eagles. We did our job."

"Don't you even care what happens to the bald eagles? They're our national symbol!"

"And they're endangered," Tracy added. "There are only thirty pairs left in the whole state." Julie smiled gratefully at her sister.

"Look, I'm sorry about the eagles, okay? All I can say is people need homes, too." He gestured out the window toward a cluster of framed-up houses. "A few birds—maybe that's the price of progress."

"Well, you took away their home—it's only fair that your company help them get a new one." Julie explained about the hack tower and the money it cost to release the eagles.

The foreman chewed his pencil for a moment. "Look, tell you what. I'll talk to the boss. Might be we could donate some scrap lumber for that tower of yours. But I'm not making any promises here."

Julie nodded. She scribbled down the phone number of the rescue center and passed it to him. "If your boss says yes, call here and ask for Robin. And thank you!"

"Like I said, no promises, kid."

❖

The next afternoon, Julie bounced into Robin's office. She couldn't wait to tell Robin about the visit to Mountain Meadow Homes. But Robin sat slumped at her desk, her head in her hands.

"Have a seat, Julie," she murmured before Julie had said a word.

Julie sat down, feeling uncertain. Finally Robin looked up. "We lost one of the baby eagles last night."

Julie hesitated. "Do you want me to help look for it?" she asked.

"Julie," Robin said gently, "the baby eagle died."

"But I just . . . it was . . . how could that happen?" Julie took in a ragged breath, tears beginning to smart.

"We found it this morning, on the floor of the cage," said Robin. "We're not exactly sure what happened. It could have fallen. But I think it has more to do with being in captivity. Shasta and Sierra can't care for their babies the way they would in the wild."

Julie stared at her hands. Her eyes welled with tears.

"I know how you feel," Robin comforted her. "This is the hardest part of my job."

Julie nodded in sympathy. "How's the other baby doing?"

"It's going to need extra care and attention. We'll hand-feed it for a while and monitor it closely."

"Can I see it?" Julie asked.

"Tell you what," said Robin, glancing at her watch. "It's about time for her feeding, and you can help." Robin took a metal bowl out of a large refrigerator.

Julie wrinkled her nose. "Smells fishy."

"That's what it is—fish, chopped into bite-size pieces." Robin took something that looked like an eagle head from a shelf in the workroom. Slipping it over her hand, she made the yellow beak snap open and shut.

Julie's eyes widened. "A bald eagle puppet? It looks just like Shasta and Sierra!"

Robin nodded. "We'll feed the eaglet with this, so that she thinks she's getting food from another eagle. If she imprints to a human, we won't be able to let her go in the wild." Robin put her finger up to her lips. "Watch me first. Then you can take a turn," she whispered.

Julie peered into the nest, which was now in a

separate cage. The eaglet looked like a fuzzy ball of lint—tufts of dark gray down with tiny feathers sprouting all over, like white freckles.

With the puppet, Robin scooped up a beakful of fish and reached toward the nest. The baby eagle hungrily snatched the fish scraps out of the puppet's beak. After Robin had fed the eaglet several bites of fish, she whispered, "Want to give it a try?"

Julie nodded, too much in awe to speak. She slipped the bald eagle puppet over her hand, inserting her thumb and fingers into its beak. She scooped up a piece of fish—and dropped it. The baby's dark eyes watched the puppet's every move. Its beak snapped at the bald eagle puppet, looking for food. After a few tries, Julie got the hang of it, and soon the nestling was greedily gulping down every morsel she offered.

Once Julie was comfortable, Robin left her to finish the feeding on her own. Julie felt pleased to be helping. If Shasta and Sierra couldn't take care of their baby, she and Robin would give it extra-special care and attention.

Julie couldn't help thinking about the eaglet that had died. There was nothing she could do to save

that one now. But at least she could feed this one, and it would have a fighting chance.

When every last scrap of fish was gone, the scruffy eaglet snuggled down into its nest, fluffing its speckled down.

"Don't you worry—you're gonna make it," Julie whispered. "We're counting on you, Freckles."

CHAPTER
FOUR

EARTH DAY

On Monday at school, Julie's thoughts kept returning to Shasta, Sierra, and Freckles. She drew a bald eagle flying in the margin of her science notebook. Then she doodled the letters *S A V E* and filled in the words *Save All Vanishing Eagles*. It chilled her to think that all over California—all over the country—bald eagles were losing their homes and their lives. Surely if people realized this, they'd stop it from happening.

Julie's teacher, Ms. Hunter, walked to the front of the room and cleared her throat. "Class, who can tell me what special day is coming up?"

Julie's hand shot up. "Earth Day! It's on April twenty-second. And this Saturday, there's going to be a big celebration in Golden Gate Park."

"That's right," said Ms. Hunter. "Now, what can we do as a class to help planet Earth?"

"We could recycle the used paper from our classroom," said Kimberly.

"Good. What else?" asked Ms. Hunter.

"I saw on TV how fish and ocean birds die from eating plastic trash," said Jeff. "We could pick up litter on the beach."

"Another good suggestion. Any more ideas?"

Julie told the class about the bald eagles at the rescue center. "And it's going to cost at least a thousand dollars to release the eagles back into the wild," she added.

"Helping bald eagles would be cool," said Julie's friend T. J. Everyone agreed and began thinking up ways to raise money—bake sales, car washes, lemonade stands.

Ms. Hunter clapped her hands to quiet the hubbub. "Can we think of a way to not only raise money but also raise *awareness* about how bald eagles are endangered?" she asked.

"There are only thirty nesting pairs of bald eagles left in all of California," Julie told the class. "If people knew that, I'm sure they'd want to help."

"We could launch sixty balloons on Earth Day," said Alison. "One for each bald eagle left in California."

"Wow! Great idea," everybody agreed.

"I think we're onto something here," Ms. Hunter said. "But what happens to all those balloons after they go up?"

"Oh, yeah," said Jeff. "Balloons pop and end up littering."

"How about sixty kites, then?" asked Alison.

"We could fly them on Earth Day all at once and tell everybody what's happening to the bald eagles," Amanda added.

"My mom owns a shop," said Julie. "Maybe she could order some kites."

"How are we going to raise money by flying kites?" Kenneth asked.

The room grew quiet. At last Julie said, "How about if you donate five dollars, you get a kite to fly."

The room buzzed with excitement.

"Class, this sounds like an excellent activity for Earth Day," said Ms. Hunter. "What shall we call our project?"

T. J. reached over and held up Julie's notebook. "How about Project SAVE, for Save All Vanishing Eagles?"

Ms. Hunter wrote the name in block letters across the blackboard. Looking around the room, Julie felt a surge of pride in her classmates. It was true—people really *did* care about helping the bald eagles. But first they had to know about the problem.

As soon as school let out, Julie raced home. Instead of heading upstairs to the apartment for a snack, as she usually did, she went straight into Gladrags, her mom's shop on the ground floor. When Julie described her class project, Mom agreed to order the kites and donate them to Project SAVE.

"I think I've even seen some kites that have pictures of eagles printed on them," said Mom, handing Julie a catalogue.

Leafing through the catalogue, Julie found the eagle kites. They came in ready-to-assemble kits. Perfect! She couldn't wait to tell Robin.

Suddenly, Julie had another idea. She gave her

mom a quick hug, ran upstairs, shoved her tape recorder into her backpack, then hopped onto her bike. If she made it to the rescue center by four o'clock, she'd be there in time to feed Freckles.

Robin's face lit up when Julie told her about Project SAVE. "Kites are a great idea. Why don't we set up an extra table at the Randall Museum's booth and have kids make the kites right there? That would be a great Earth Day activity. And we'll put up a sign thanking Gladrags for donating the kites."

Julie pulled the tape recorder from her backpack. "I was thinking we could play eagle sounds over a loudspeaker at the booth, too. Is it okay for me to tape Shasta and Sierra?"

"That'll sure get everyone's attention," said Robin. "Listen, they're screeching right now."

Kweek kuk kuk, kweek-a-kuk kuk! The harsh cries always gave Julie a thrill of excitement. The calls sounded fierce and wild, just like the eagles. Julie switched her tape player to record and set it outside the eagle cage.

Then it was time to feed Freckles. Julie put on the bald eagle puppet, but when she held out a scrap of fish, Freckles did not snap her beak to take it. In fact, she barely raised her head to look at the puppet.

Julie rushed down the hall to tell Robin.

"That's weird," said Robin. "I haven't fed her since early this morning. She should be hungry."

Robin followed Julie back to the eagle room. "Her eyes look clear," she said, peering at Freckles. "And she has plenty of water, so she shouldn't be dehydrated. She's not shaking or shivering. I don't know what's wrong."

Julie couldn't help thinking of the other baby eagle. "She's not going to die, is she?"

"I hope not," said Robin.

"Maybe she wants to be back in the cage with Shasta and Sierra," said Julie.

"Could be. Sometimes it's hard to figure out what's wrong when birds aren't in their natural environment," said Robin. "I'd better call the vet."

Julie stared helplessly at the little eaglet, willing her to get well. She imagined a day when Freckles, with full-fledged feathers, would soar wild and free high above the treetops. Would that day ever come?

Robin poked her head in. "Julie, your mom just

called and wants you home for dinner."

"But Freckles—"

Robin put her hand on Julie's shoulder. "You can't stay here all night with Freckles. The vet's on his way. You've done all you can do."

"I just don't want to come back tomorrow and find her . . ." Julie couldn't finish her sentence.

Robin shrugged helplessly. "I know, Julie. I know."

Saturday morning, Julie woke to the crunch of a shovel breaking new ground outside her second-story window. Arm-wrestling the window open, she peered down.

Hank, a family friend from the neighborhood, looked up from his digging and waved. He was wearing an owl T-shirt that said *Give a Hoot, Don't Pollute*, and he was smiling under his bushy red beard.

"What are you up to?" Julie asked from her perch.

"We're planting trees along Haight Street for Earth Day," Hank called back.

"This one was left over, and I thought it might spruce up the front of Gladrags. It's a red-flowering gum tree." Delicate branches covered with pink blossoms swayed in the light wind. The new tree looked as if it was waving, too.

"It looks great," Julie called. "I'm off to Golden Gate Park for the big celebration. Happy Earth Day!"

"Have fun!" Hank called back.

Golden Gate Park hummed with activity. The happy rhythm of calypso music pulsed from a stage. Paint-splattered teenagers created a mural splashed with suns and rainbows, whales and ocean waves. Julie made her way down the row of exhibit booths, collecting buttons with slogans like *Save the Whales* and *Every Day Is Earth Day*.

When she found the Randall Museum booth, Robin was setting up a table for the kite-making area. "You're just in time to help me cover this table with paper," said Robin. "Then we'll put out scissors and tape."

"Okay, but first—tell me, what did the vet say today about Freckles?" It had been several days since the vet had taken Freckles in for observation.

"Good news. She's eating again, and we'll probably get her back by Monday. But Dr. Ingram says if we don't get these birds up into the hack tower within the next two weeks, Freckles may never be able to join her parents or live as a wild bird."

Julie swallowed. "Let's hope the kites are a big hit."

"I got this big pickle jar, and I thought we could put it out today for donations," said Robin, setting the jar on the table.

Julie dug deep into her pocket and pulled out a wrinkled bill. "I'm donating the first five dollars. That way the jar won't look so empty."

Soon T. J. and Ms. Hunter showed up to help at the kite-making table. Ivy and her brother, Andrew, were their first customers.

"Five-dollar donation! Make a kite!" T. J. shouted, cupping his hands into a megaphone.

"Save the bald eagles," Julie called out. Soon kids and families crowded around the table, putting their kites together and attaching tails and strings. Julie talked with people of all ages, passing out information and answering questions.

"Save the bald eagles," Julie called out.

A lady in a straw hat picked up one of the flyers. "Bald eagles!" she said to Julie. "I'm a bird-watcher, and I used to see them from our ranch not so many years ago. But I'm afraid I haven't seen an eagle for quite some time."

"Where's your ranch?" Julie asked curiously.

"Near the coast, in Marin County." The woman looked up from the flyer, and Julie thought she recognized the friendly blue eyes under the wide-brimmed straw hat.

"Hey! Aren't you the butterfly lady?" Julie asked. The woman furrowed her brow. "Remember? That day at the Conservatory—you told me about the blue butterfly that landed on my shoulder."

The lady's blue eyes crinkled with recognition. "So you're the butterfly girl," she said, smiling broadly. "I'm Mrs. Mildred Woodacre. So glad to meet you again."

"I'm Julie Albright," said Julie, and soon the two were chatting like old friends. Julie told her how finding the baby owl that day had led to becoming a volunteer at the rescue center. And she was happy to report that the vet had said the baby screech owl was pulling through.

"What a pretty T-shirt," said Mrs. Woodacre. "Why, it has an eagle on it!"

"My dad got it for me to wear today," Julie said proudly. "Isn't it boss?" She chattered on, telling Mrs. Woodacre the whole story of Shasta, Sierra, and Freckles. "That's why I'm here today," she finished. "We have to raise enough money for the eagles to be released, or they'll live in a cage for the rest of their lives."

"Oh, my," Mrs. Woodacre said softly, putting a hand to her chest. "It just breaks my heart to think of any wild creature living out its life in a cage."

"Hey, Julie," T. J. called. "We've got sixty done— time to launch the kites."

❁

Julie and Ivy picked up the kite they had assembled and made their way over to the grassy meadow not far from the Conservatory. A small crowd of kids and parents gathered atop the hill at the far end of the meadow. Ms. Hunter was helping a group of Julie's classmates get ready to launch their kites.

"Look," said T. J., all out of breath from running.

"TV cameras! Ms. Hunter says the KSKY news channel is here for Earth Day. Maybe our kites will be on TV!"

"Then we'd better get them up in the air," said Julie.

"Happy Earth Day," Robin announced. A TV cameraman moved in and pointed the camera right at her, but she did not seem nervous. "Welcome to the Randall Museum's bald eagle kite-flying extravaganza! It's a sad fact that our national symbol, the bald eagle, is rapidly disappearing. Today, thanks to all of you, every kite we send up into the air helps toward the release of three bald eagles at our rescue center." Everybody clapped, and Robin made a final pitch for sending donations to the rescue center. "And now, the girl who helped bring all this about— Julie Albright!"

Taking hold of the microphone, Julie said, "First, I'd like to thank my family, my friends, my teacher, Ms. Hunter, and my whole class at Jack London Elementary School for coming up with this idea and helping to make it happen." Julie's class went wild, whooping and cheering.

A bright light shone on Julie. The camera was

pointed at her now. She squinted into the glare, took a deep breath, and said, "Today, sixty eagle kites will fly in the sky—one for each of the bald eagles that have nests in the state of California. With your help, we hope that three real bald eagles will have a chance—a chance to return to the wild, where they belong. Happy Earth Day, everybody. Let's go fly a kite!"

As Julie bent to pick up her kite, a man with a spiral notebook who had been talking to Robin asked, "Julie Albright? Can I get the correct spelling of your name and your age?"

"Hey," said T. J. excitedly. "Aren't you the weatherman from Channel 12?"

"That's me, Joe Smiley," said the man. "I've been out here all day covering Earth Day."

"Told ya!" said T. J., bouncing on his toes. "Hey, make that foghorn sound you do every morning."

"No, say that thing you always say when it's raining," said Ivy.

"It's raining catfish and frogs out there this morning," said Mr. Smiley in a deep voice. "Better take the boat to work." A bunch of kids gathered around, laughing.

"Is Smiley your real name, Mr. Smiley?" asked another of Julie's classmates.

"Sure is," said the weatherman with a grin.

"Is Julie going to be on TV?" Ivy asked.

"Can't say for sure," said Mr. Smiley. "But we shot a nice clip back there. It just might fit into our Earth Day segment on the six o'clock news." He motioned to the cameraman. "Let's roll!"

Julie and Ivy raced to the top of the grassy hill. Ivy held the kite high above her head. Holding the reel of string, Julie let out about four feet and with a "Ready, set, go!" took off running down the hill. Ivy let go of the kite, and up, up, up it went. The eagle kite rose on an updraft, high as a tree, until a sudden gust sent it sideways, dipping toward the ground. Julie ran and the kite rose again, catching the strong breeze.

In no time, people of all ages were whooping with delight as their kites lifted off the ground. Julie let out some more string, and her kite soared high, joining the other kites, where they dipped and fluttered, gathering far overhead like

an aerie of eagles, white against the blue sky. Julie
tilted her head, squinting against the bright rays of
the sun until she could see the dark silhouette of the
eagle on her kite. Julie imagined it to be Shasta or
Sierra, swooping and soaring way up in the sky.

"This is your eagle-eye reporter, Julie Albright,"
coming to you live from Golden Gate Park." Julie
spoke clearly into her ketchup-bottle microphone.

"Shh, here it is," said Tracy, pointing at the
television. Mom, Tracy, and Julie glued their eyes to
the six o'clock news on the screen.

Joe Smiley came on. "That's the guy! The one
who talked to Robin and me," said Julie. Joe talked
about the mayor's Earth Day speech, a mural painted
to beautify a playground, and efforts to start curbside
recycling in the city. Julie jumped up and pointed.
"There's Robin. She's asking for donations to the
rescue center."

Just when Julie thought they were going to a
commercial break, Joe Smiley said, "One nine-year-
old, Julie Albright, is working hard to save our
national bird." The camera panned to Julie.

"There you are!" screamed Tracy.

"You're on TV!" said Mom, leaning in closer.

"This young activist believes *you* can make a difference," said Joe Smiley, pointing his finger at the camera. "To help save the bald eagles, send your donation to the address on the screen."

"Robin will be so happy that they told everybody where to send money," Julie said after the segment ended. "She says we're almost out of time for the eagle release."

"I'm proud of you, honey," said Mom, giving her a sideways squeeze.

Just then the phone rang. Dad had seen Julie on the news, too. They chatted, and then Julie hung up and came back into the living room.

"So, how's it feel to be famous?" Tracy asked.

"I was only on for two seconds," said Julie.

"So? Two seconds of fame is still famous."

"Thanks," said Julie. "But it's the bald eagles that I hope will be famous. Famous for flying free again."

TRYING TO FLY

On Tuesday after school, Julie biked straight to the rescue center. She thought of the pickle jar chock-full of coins and dollar bills on Earth Day. The bald eagles had even been mentioned on TV! *Shasta and Sierra will surely be released now,* thought Julie.

Julie poked her head into Robin's office. "So, are we going to get that hack tower built?"

Robin looked up and smiled, but she didn't have the upbeat expression that Julie was expecting. "I've counted the money twice," said Robin. "We raised three hundred dollars from the kites, and another forty-two dollars from the donations in the pickle jar. But we still come up way short."

Julie frowned, doing the math in her head. "To reach a thousand dollars, we need another . . . six hundred fifty-eight dollars." She paused, sobered by the large number. "Well, now that it's been on the news, I bet people will send in all kinds of money."

"We have had a few donations already," said Robin, "but only small amounts so far—nothing like what we need. If we don't have the money by Friday, Fish and Wildlife can't start building the tower next week. And we just can't wait any longer."

"But—" Julie scuffed the leg of the table with the toe of her shoe.

"I'm sorry, Julie. After all your hard work, I know this isn't what you wanted to hear."

"Shasta and Sierra can't go to a zoo now," said Julie. "It's just not right."

Robin sighed. "Listen, would you do me a big favor and feed Freckles? That always cheers you up."

Julie nodded and headed down the hall. Freckles needed her, and that's what she had to fix her mind on for the moment.

Freckles was feisty and growing bigger by the day. Hungrier than usual, she gulped down the fish in no time. Julie was just washing off the eagle puppet when she heard a voice call out, "Yoo-hoo! Anybody here?" Julie hurried out of the workroom and saw a white-haired woman in a familiar straw hat.

"Mrs. Woodacre! Hi," Julie said. "Are you here to see Shasta and Sierra?"

"I most certainly am," said Mrs. Woodacre. "After hearing about your bald eagles on Earth Day, I had to come and see them for myself."

"I'll be your tour guide." Julie motioned for Mrs. Woodacre to follow her.

Julie stopped in front of the big cage. The two huge eagles sat motionless on their perches, fixing their audience with the fierce gaze that always gave Julie the shivers. She and Mrs. Woodacre watched in humbled silence.

"Aren't they amazing?" Julie whispered.

"Magnificent," Mrs. Woodacre said softly.

In the blink of an eye, Shasta threw back his head and let out a piercing screech. Hopping off his perch, he lifted into the air, beating his wings furiously, then glided to the floor.

"Whoa—he flew!" Julie gasped.

"He must be testing his wings," said Mrs. Woodacre.

"I bet his injured wing is all healed now. Let's go tell Robin he's trying to fly."

"That was quite a show!" said Mrs. Woodacre as they returned to the front office. "Now, I can't leave without one of those eagle kites. I'm going to fly it at the ranch when my grandson comes to visit."

"We have a few extras left over from Earth Day," said Julie. "I'll go get one."

While Mrs. Woodacre chatted with Robin about the eagles, Julie riffled through the boxes from Earth Day. "Here," said Julie, handing a kite kit to Mrs. Woodacre. "All you need are tape and scissors. It's pretty easy."

"Sounds fine," said Mrs. Woodacre.

"And, uh—we're asking five dollars for the kites," Julie added awkwardly.

"Well, then, good thing I brought my checkbook today," Mrs. Woodacre said with a wink. Unsnapping her pocketbook, she filled out a check and handed it to Julie.

"Thanks," said Julie. "I hope you have fun flying kites with your grandson." She started to hand the check to Robin, then stopped. Something wasn't right.

"I think you made a mistake," she said slowly.

"There are too many zeros."

"No mistake," said Mrs. Woodacre, smiling.

Julie took in a breath. "Five hundred dollars! For real?" She clutched the check to her chest.

"Bald eagles were a part of my childhood," said Mrs. Woodacre. "I hope they'll be around for generations."

"I can't tell you how much we appreciate this," said Robin, shaking Mrs. Woodacre's hand. "We were hundreds of dollars short for the eagle release, but now . . . thank you!"

After Mrs. Woodacre left, Julie turned to Robin. "Does this mean . . ." she began, almost afraid to hope.

Robin bit her lip. "We're *so* close now, but—" Suddenly she smacked her fist into her palm, as if she'd reached a decision. "I'm going to call Fish and Wildlife right now and see if they'll give us the go-ahead even though we're still a hundred fifty dollars short." Just as Robin reached for the phone, it rang.

"Randall Museum rescue center," she said, picking it up. "Yes, this is Robin Young . . . Who? You have what? Scrap lumber? Oh . . . Yes, that young lady was right. We *do* need to build a tower . . . Yes!

We'll take it, definitely. Thanks so much!"

Robin hung up the phone and gave Julie a stunned look. Then she held out her arms and picked Julie right up off the ground in a big bear hug.

HAPPY BIRTHDAY,
JULIE!

You Are Invited
Come celebrate
Julie's 10th Birthday
and watch the bald
eagle release!
WHO: Julie Albright with Shasta,
Sierra, and Freckles
WHAT: Bald Eagle Birthday
Beach Party
WHERE: Muir Beach
WHEN: May 1, 1976 - 12 p.m.
B.Y.O.B.B.
(Bring Your Own Beach Blanket)

Using her best cursive, Julie finished filling out the last of her party invitations. She double-checked her list:

Mom
Dad
Tracy
Ivy
J. J.
Robin
Mrs. Woodacre

Good, she had made seven invitations. Julie left two on the kitchen table for Mom and Tracy and then headed outside.

At the rescue center, Julie leaned in the doorway, looking all around. In just a month it had become like a second home to her. And now Robin and the eagles were going to be part of her birthday—the most important part.

Julie's heart skipped a beat, imagining the moment, less than a week away. For days, Shasta had been testing his wings every chance he got.

"Do you think Shasta's ready to fly?" Julie asked Robin as she handed her an invitation.

Robin nodded. "He's ready."

"Will the hack tower be built in time?"

"Don't you worry, birthday girl," said Robin. "Fish and Wildlife has a crew already working on it. They'll have it up before the weekend. That gives us a few days to get the eagles used to their new home before we open the door and let them fly."

"But what about Freckles? Will Shasta and Sierra know what to do once they're back in the wild?"

"That's the sixty-four-thousand-dollar question. There's a lot we don't know about releasing eagles. We won't be able to hand-feed Freckles anymore, but we'll make sure she has enough food until Shasta and Sierra start hunting again."

"I can't wait," said Julie. "I feel like *I* could fly!"

⁂

The San Francisco Bay sparkled as Julie and her family crossed the Golden Gate Bridge. She rolled the window down, letting the wind whip her hair.

"Happy birthday, world," Julie called out the window.

"I can't believe my little girl's turning ten years old," said Mom as they turned off the highway and headed toward the beach on California Route One.

"Yeah! Double digits!" said Julie.

"Quiet, everybody—I love this song," said Tracy.

"Hey, it's the Eagles! Turn up the radio," Julie urged. She and Ivy joined in from the back seat, singing at the top of their lungs.

Put me-e-e on a highway
And sho-ow me a sign,
And take it to the limit one more ti-i-i-ime.

They threaded their way up and over Mount Tamalpais on a ribbon of road that wound its way through lofty redwood trees toward the coast.

"We're here!" Julie shouted, scrambling to be first out of the car.

"Wait up!" yelled Tracy. "Just 'cause it's your birthday doesn't mean you don't have to help carry stuff."

Arms full, they made their way down a path edged with wild purple lupine and fiery Indian paintbrush. Julie and Ivy ripped off their shoes and ran to the water's edge, daring to stick their toes in the icy-cold Pacific. They squealed in delight as ocean waves crashed up over their ankles.

Soon Dad and the others were arriving, and introductions were made all around. Tracy helped Dad build a campfire, while Mrs. Woodacre helped Mom set out the food. Julie and T. J. tossed a Frisbee, starting a game of keep-away from Robin and Ivy. Before long, everybody was feasting on chicken kebabs and potato salad and sipping lemonade.

When the picnic was over, Dad handed Julie a present. "I know we said we'd wait to open presents back at home, but I have one that couldn't wait. You'll see why."

Julie tore off the wrapping. "Binoculars!"

"Happy birthday, honey," said Dad.

"Thanks,"Julie said, throwing her arms around him. "It's almost time," she exclaimed, looking up at the hack tower through her binoculars.

Robin checked her watch. "The guys from Fish and Wildlife said they'll open the cage at two o'clock. But that doesn't mean the eagles will fly as soon as the door is opened. So don't get your hopes up too high."

"Too late for that," said Tracy. "Julie's hopes are already sky-high." Everyone laughed.

"Will the baby eagle fly, too?" T. J. asked.

"Freckles isn't old enough to fly yet," Robin explained. "She's only about eight weeks old. In a few more weeks, when she's fully fledged out, she'll be able to leave the tower, too."

Julie passed around her binoculars, and the others took turns getting the hack tower into view.

"I see them!" said Ivy. "One of the big eagles is flapping all around inside the tower."

"Let me see," said Julie, peering through the binoculars. "That's Sierra. You can always tell the female because she's bigger than the male. And hey, it looks as if she's preening Freckles."

At two o'clock, a hush fell over the gathering. Everyone waited, heads tilted back, eyes glued to the spot at the top of the headland cliffs. Julie held her breath. The only sound was the crashing of the waves.

"Nothing's happening," she said impatiently. "Dad, what time is it?"

"It's only been ten minutes," said Dad.

"Feels like an hour," said T. J.

"Feels like forever," said Julie.

"We have to be patient," said Robin. "Remember, they may not even fly today at all."

Julie held her breath. The only sound was the crashing of the waves.

After a while, Mom started packing up the picnic basket.

"Maybe they're just not ready yet," said Dad. "Even pilots have days they don't feel like flying," he joked, with a wink at Julie.

But Julie was too anxious to smile back. "Ten more minutes," she pleaded. She picked up the binoculars and pointed them at the hack tower one more time. "Wait—I think I see something moving. It's Sierra. She came out! She just hopped onto the perch pole on the tower."

"And there's Shasta, right behind her," said Ivy, who was looking through Dad's field glasses.

The two eagles flapped and jumped, and then rose up off the platform and perched on top of the hack tower. Mom and Mrs. Woodacre clapped.

"C'mon, Shasta. C'mon, Sierra," T. J. called. "You can do it."

"Fly!" Julie cried. "Fly!"

Suddenly there was a great flapping of wings and several loud screeches. *Kree! Kree!* Sierra launched off the perch pole, circled the tower once, and landed on the branch of a windswept cypress tree. *Krr-eee! Krr-eee!* Sierra called to Shasta to join her. Shasta leapt off the tower, swooping and gliding, and landed next to his mate.

The two birds lingered a moment. Then, in a whoosh of wings, they flew back in unison and perched again on the hack tower.

"They did it—they flew!" said Julie, jumping up and down.

"That short test flight is probably it for now," said Robin. "Especially with Shasta's injured wing."

"Maybe they need more practice," said Julie. "Practice being free."

Before she could say another word, Shasta glided off the hack tower, out into open space, out over the beach beyond the cliff. Julie and the others watched silently, breathlessly. Even without binoculars he was clearly visible, a speck high above, looping gracefully across the sky.

Suddenly, without warning, Shasta began tumbling in a tailspin toward the ground.

"*Nooooo!*" Julie shouted, waving her arms and running down the beach. Sierra flew out and hovered in the air above her mate, screeching and calling to Shasta.

Halfway down the beach, Julie stood frozen,

watching the drama unfold. She could not take her eyes off Shasta as he spiraled toward the ground. *Fly, Shasta, fly*, she pleaded in silent prayer. She raised outstretched hands. If only she could break his fall, lift him back up on the wind.

Just when she could hardly bear to watch, a strong gust filled Shasta's wings, lifting him up and up. A chorus of cheers and hoorays resounded from below. Julie raced back to her friends and family, sand flying. "He did it. He's going to make it!" She trained her binoculars back on the hack tower. "Hey, Freckles hopped over to the doorway. She's watching, too."

Shasta had joined Sierra now. As Julie watched in silent admiration, the eagle pair took wing out over the ocean, soaring on the wind.

LOOKING BACK

CARING FOR THE EARTH
IN THE
1970s

In Julie's time, Americans were starting to understand that nature—the plants and animals, the air and water—needed protection from people. America's forests, rivers, and coastlines seemed so vast, it was hard to imagine that human activity could cause lasting damage. But as people gained awareness of serious problems like air and water pollution, they began to see that simply setting natural areas aside in parks and preserves was not enough to protect them from harm.

A few years before Julie was born, a biologist and writer named Rachel Carson wrote a book, *Silent Spring*, which showed that chemical pollution was causing serious problems in the environment. Pesticides such as DDT, which killed crop-eating insects and

Rachel Carson

disease-carrying mosquitoes, had been viewed as safe and were widely used. But Rachel Carson explained that when insects ate DDT-sprayed plants, the poison remained in the insects' bodies. Animals that ate the insects died or developed health problems, and animals that ate *those* animals were also affected.

The effects, although long-lasting, were sometimes hard to detect. When birds ate insects or other creatures that had eaten DDT, their eggshells became so thin that they broke when the mother bird sat on her nest, and the birds couldn't reproduce. Even baby birds that hatched successfully often became sick, as Julie found with the baby owl. But it took many years before scientists knew that DDT was hurting birds.

An Earth Day banner

When Americans realized their activities were harming the natural world, they began passing laws to protect it. After *Silent Spring* came out, Congress passed the Clean Air Act of 1963 and, a few years later, created the Environmental Protection Agency. In 1970, Americans celebrated the first Earth Day with fairs and activities to clean up and educate their communities.

In New York, girls cleaned trash from the sidewalks on Earth Day, 1970.

In 1972, Congress banned DDT and passed the Endangered Species Act, making it illegal to kill endangered animals and plants or to disturb their habitats. When companies wanted to build a dam or cut down trees in a wilderness area, first the area had to be studied to see if any endangered species lived there. If the study found that the project would disturb endangered plants or animals, then it could not move ahead. Some citizens disliked this new law, but most people felt that protecting the natural world was as important as having clean air and water.

Kids in the '70s worried about air and water pollution. Sidewalk chalk was one way kids could send a public message!

Like Julie, Americans were deeply saddened to learn that their nation's symbol, the bald eagle, was one of the species in danger of extinction. DDT was not the eagles' only problem. With their seven-foot wingspans, bald eagles flew into power lines and were electrocuted. They ate animals wounded by lead shot from hunters and got lead poisoning. And they were running out of places

This wildlife rescue worker educates the public about bald eagles.

to nest. Bald eagles live in tall trees near oceans, lakes, or rivers—valuable real estate where people like to have homes. Around the time of Julie's story, a survey found only 708 breeding pairs of bald eagles in the entire mainland United States.

Today, the bald eagle is one of the environmental movement's biggest successes. Through the protections of the Endangered Species Act and the efforts of wildlife biologists and countless volunteers like Julie and Robin, the bald eagle has made a comeback. In 2006, around 8,000 bald eagle pairs were breeding in the mainland U.S. and more in Alaska, and the bald eagle was scheduled to be taken off the federal Endangered Species list.

Success stories like the bald eagle show what people can accomplish when the government, scientists, environmental organizations such as the Sierra Club, and individual citizens all work together. But the natural world still faces many threats from human activity, and trying to save a plant or animal species sometimes creates other problems. In the early 1990s, 30,000

loggers in Washington and Oregon lost their jobs when the northern spotted owl received protection under the Endangered Species Act.

Northern spotted owl

Loggers protested when their work was stopped to protect the northern spotted owl.

A few years later, in California's Headwaters Forest, a young woman named Julia Butterfly Hill climbed up a 200-foot-tall redwood tree that was going to be logged. For two long years, through freezing winters with lightning, hailstorms, and high winds, Julia lived in the tree to protect it from being cut down. The 1000-year-old redwood, nicknamed Luna, was part of a rare remnant of old-growth forest that was being clearcut, causing great damage to the forest, hillside, and houses nearby. Ten years of organized protests and legal efforts had not stopped the logging. From her perch high in Luna's branches, Julia used a cell phone to talk to reporters as well as the lumber company president, who even visited her up in the tree. At last, Julia persuaded the lumber company to spare Luna and the surrounding trees.

Julia lived in a makeshift tent on a wooden platform 180 feet up—that's as high as a 12-story building! She wanted the logging company—and the public—to view the trees as rare and ancient living things, not just as valuable lumber.

In clearcut logging, every tree is cut down. Clearcuts often cause mudslides that pollute rivers and even destroy people's—as well as animals'—homes.

As the human population grows and scientists learn more about the impact our activities have on the natural world, these struggles over the environment will continue. Some people feel it is wrong to place more importance on saving a bird or a tree than on saving people's jobs and livelihoods. Others believe that because America's natural environment is shared and inherited by all Americans, now and in the future, it deserves the very best protection we can give it.

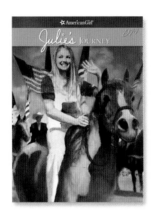

It's summer, and Julie joins her cousins on a wagon train for the Bicentennial. At first, life on a covered wagon is a blast, but Julie finds out that traveling by horsepower isn't all fun and games.

*J*une 18

*More wagons join us
every day. This morning April
and I counted forty-one wagons in
our wagon train.*

*Around noon we arrived in the
town of Bakersville. The high-school marching band led us
through the town, and hundreds of people lined the streets
to cheer us on. It was sort of a parade. My arm aches from
waving so much!*

As the days passed, Julie settled into the rhythm of
life on a wagon train. Each morning, Aunt Catherine
made oatmeal and hot chocolate for breakfast. After
breakfast, Julie packed up her bedding and helped
April and Tracy take down their small tent. While
Uncle Buddy harnessed Mack and Molly, the girls
helped Aunt Catherine load the wagon. Then they
all climbed aboard, waving good-bye to Jimmy as he
rode off to join the outriders, and took their place in
the line of wagons moving slowly out onto the road.

The June weather was fine and sunny, with a
welcome breeze that kept the horses from overheating.
The girls usually started out riding with their legs

hanging out the back, watching the scenery go by. Sometimes they took turns riding up in front on the buckboard with April's parents or even walked alongside the wagon to stretch their legs. One afternoon a thunderstorm blew up. The sky darkened, and Aunt Catherine quickly drew the canvas cover closed. The three girls sat cosily on the floor of the wagon, listening to the rain patter on the canvas cover and giggling about everything and nothing. Julie had never heard anyone laugh as much as her cousin April! Just hearing April giggle made Julie crack up, even when she had no idea what the joke was. And the girls didn't mind the rain. It gave them a chance to play cards and board games and Twenty Questions. The hours slipped by in a rhythm as steady as Mack's and Molly's hoofbeats.

At midday the wagon train usually stopped in a park or field where the horses could graze. While Tracy helped Aunt Catherine prepare lunch, Julie and April liked to wander among the wagons, saying hello to the other people and horses, and each trying to be the first to spot Jimmy and Hurricane. One day they found Jimmy hunched over his saddle fixing a stirrup strap. Hurricane was tied to a nearby tree.

Jimmy looked up as the girls approached. "April, would you mind taking Hurricane down to the stream for a drink? He's cooled off now." Jimmy had warned Julie that you couldn't water a horse that was still hot and sweaty—the horse could get sick.

April nodded. "Sure. C'mon, Julie." She untied Hurricane's rope and started across the field toward the creek. Suddenly she turned to Julie. "Hey, want to ride Hurricane? I'll boost you up."

"Really?" Julie's heart began to pound. "But wait, what about a saddle?"

"You can ride bareback," said April. "It's super fun. C'mon, I'll give you a leg up." She cupped her hands to make a foothold. Julie stepped into April's hand and in one swift motion swung her other leg up and over the horse.

"Hold on to his mane," April instructed. As April led Hurricane across the grassy field, Julie wobbled from side to side. Hurricane's bare back was slippery. She hunkered down low, clinging to the horse's mane.

"Try to relax," April coached. "Sit up straight and get your balance."

Gradually, Julie sat up a little taller, gripping the sides of the horse with her thighs. She eased into the clip-clop rocking motion of the horse, feeling his warmth against her legs, his back muscles rippling with each step.

"Good—that's it. You're getting it," said April.

"I'm really riding!" said Julie.

"You're doing great! Want to try a trot?" April asked.

"Sure, why not," said Julie.

"Here, take the rope." April tossed the end of the lead rope up to her. Julie let go of the mane with one hand and caught it.

"Now kick him with your heels," April called. She broke into a jog. "Let's go, Hurricane."

Julie swung out her feet and gave the horse a kick. Hurricane shot across the field, heading straight for the creek. *Ba-da-rump, ba-da-rump, ba-da-rump.* All Julie could hear was the beating of hooves and the whoosh of air in her ears. "Help!" she called, but April was fast falling behind.

"Hangggg onnn!" April's voice was nearly lost in

the thundering of hooves.

Julie clung desperately to Hurricane's side, one leg barely hooked over his back. She clutched at his mane. All she could see was the ground—and Hurricane's pounding hooves. Dust stung her eyes. Her heart thumped against her rib cage. If she fell, surely she'd be trampled.

Just when Julie thought she couldn't hang on another second, Hurricane came to a dead stop at the creek's edge. Julie didn't remember letting go. She didn't remember flying through the air. All she knew was the smack of cold water and the bite of a large rock under her shoulder. The wind was knocked out of her. She took in a ragged breath, scrambling backward on all fours like a crab to get away from Hurricane, who was calmly taking a drink.

"Julie, are you okay?" April asked, helping her to her feet. "Oh no, you're sopping wet. You look like a drowned rat!"

"It's not funny," said Julie. "I almost got trampled. And after I fell I could hardly even breathe."

April picked up the lead rope. "You'll be okay.

Falling is part of learning to ride. You have to fall at least seven times before you're a good rider."

"Well, forget about learning to ride, then," Julie muttered. "I'm not getting back up on that horse."

"Oh, don't be such a baby. Look, I won't let go of the rope this time, and we'll just stay at a walk."

"I'm not a baby," said Julie, but her voice came out all wobbly and her legs felt like spaghetti. They headed back across the field in silence.

"Hey Julie, just think—this is kind of like the time in *Little House on the Prairie* when Nellie fell off Laura's horse," said April.

Julie glowered at her cousin. "For your information," she snapped, "that was just in the TV show. The *real* Laura never took Nellie riding—she took her into the stream so Nellie would get leeches on her legs."

"Leeches? Eeww!" April began to giggle. But this time it didn't make Julie laugh.

June 20, after lunch

I don't care what April or anybody says. I'm not getting back on that horse—ever.

June 20, later

I re-read On the Banks of Plum Creek *for seven whole miles. Translation: I am not talking to April.*

Reading about pioneers is not the same as doing it. Riding Hurricane wasn't like what I imagined. Trying to stay on a bareback horse was harder than turning a cartwheel on the balance beam at gymnastics with Ivy. Maybe it wasn't so hard for Laura when she sat bareback on one of Pa's plow horses, but Hurricane is no plow horse, that's for sure.

Here's what's really bugging me: April thinks she knows all about horses and riding, but she should not have let go of the rope. I could have been hurt. Then she wouldn't have been laughing!

April and Tracy are taking a magazine quiz. Are you more like a marshmallow or a carrot? What a dumb question.

I miss Ivy. And Mom. And Dad. And my nice private bedroom with no dumb giggling teenagers.

I never would have made it as a pioneer. Why did I even come on this trip?

❀